MW01268560

Adventures of Laydin-locs "Grandma gets Kidnapped" Volume 1
By Jacqueline James
Published by Parables
March 2022 All Rights Reserved.
ISBN 978-1-954308-73-2 Copyright by Jacqueline James

The adventures of Laydin-locs "Grandma gets Kidnapped"

Written By: Jacqueline James

These series of books Adventures of Laydin-locs are dedicated to my youngest Granddaughter Laydin Elizabeth Haynes Bailey aka "Laydin-locs"

Laydin-locs I will always love you!

Adventures of Laydin-locs are stories of an adorable little girl named Laydin-locs.

Laydin-locs is very energetic with an overwhelming sense of curiosity. Laydin-locs also has a very vibrant imagination; and she expresses her enthusiasm throughout her days of play.

Laydin-locs has captured the heart of her grandmother during her visits, which has compelled her grandmother to share these special moments through several extravagant stories. Laydin-locs Grandmother hopes to bring enlightenment to (you) the reader hearts as well. Some of these stories were based on actual events.

   Therefore the "Adventures of Laydin-locs" series will inspire, inform, also educate (you) the readers through these captivating influential stories. The stories are presented in an entertaining manner to keep (you) the audience longing for more.

Adventures of Laydin-loc "Grandma gets Kidnapped" is volume 1 of the beginning of several intriguing stories to follow.

Stay tuned while the author "woos" (you) the readers into a euphoria of enchantment through these wonderful adventures.

This is the story of an adorable energetic little girl named Laydin-locs. On one sunny afternoon Laydin-locs went to visit her grandmother, and they sat down at the table to decide what they would like to do fun for the day. Laydin-locs suggested spending the day at the mall, "Grandma I just want to walk around different stores and do some window shopping or maybe even buy something nice", said Laydin-Locs."

Well, that is just fine Laydin-locs, but there's always a lot of people coming and going in and out of the mall all day. This can make it very easy to get lost in the crowd or possibly get kidnapped. So, we must remember to never let go of each other's hand "said Grandma.

'I promise'', said Laydin-locs.
Once they got their jackets and
Grandma got her purse and
keys and they headed out
towards the mall.

When they arrived at the mall, Grandma drove around the parking lot to find a good spot to park. When Grandma got out of the car she opened the back door to help Laydin - Locs out. However, Laydin-locs had already unlatched the seatbelt and was ready to go inside of the mall.

They held each other's hand as they walked across the parking lot to the mall entrance. Laydin-locs was so excited upon entering the mall, that she wanted desperately to run, but she remembered that she had to hold her grandma's hand, because grandma could not keep up with her. So, she walked in a slow pace alongside her grandma holding her hand.

The first store that they walked past was a jewelry store, with a lot of gold and silver rings and necklaces. Also, an assortment of beautiful pendants and lots of other sparkling and shiny things to admire.

They walked a little more and came to a women's clothing store. The mannequins in the window were dressed in elegant clothing. Grandma had noticed one of the outfits hanging on a rack was her favorite color. But as she stared to walk towards the mannequin to get a better look, Laydin- locs got distracted by a giant bubble gum machine.

"Wow" said Laydin-Locs, as she let go of her grandmother's hand and dashed towards the bubble gum machine. She was totally mesmerized. "Pink that's my favorite, but it's all the way at the top. I know that if I ask my grandma for a quarter, she will give me one to buy it. Oh, it's so many other colors that will have to come first before the pink one.

The yellow one for lemon flavor. The red one for the cherry flavor. The blue one for the blueberry flavor. The green one for the lime flavor. The orange one for the orange flavor. The white one for the spearmint flavor. Oh, let me see how many quarters I am going to need to ask my grandma for so I can get my favorite one pink for the strawberry flavor?

As she counted on her fingers 1...2...3 Grandma…Grandma, Grandma!", screamed Laydin-Locs as she looked around and her eyes began to fill with tears. She had let go of her grandma's hand, and Grandma was nowhere in sight.

A man in the mall had approached Laydin Loc while she was screaming for her grandma." What's wrong little girl, can I help you?". "No!!" Screamed Laydin-Locs, "I don't know who you are. You are a stranger and my grandmother said do not talk to strangers".

Then a woman approached
Laydin-Locs, but Laydin-locs
refused her help as well.

Finally, when a police officer arrived after hearing the commotion. Laydin-locs shouted" Please help me, someone took my grandma!".

"I can help you find your grandma, but first I need for you to calm down and tell me her name, and describe what she is wearing", stated the officer."

Her name is Grandma, and she has on a black jacket, black pants, and some black boots and her purse is black. She is short, brown and round with big black puffy hair" said Laydin-locs after she took a deep breath to regain her composure. Please, please, please sir find my grandma.

The officer immediately got on the louder speaker to be heard around the entire mall including the parking lot, and announced, "Attention all shoppers please be informed that there's a little girl named Laydin-locs whose grandma was possibly kidnapped.

She is short and brown wearing a black jacket, black pants, black boots, with big black puffy hair and is also carrying a black purse.

Her name is _____and she will answer to grandma. If you see her, please contact the mall police office at once.

Meanwhile on the parking lot of the mall, there was a little girl pulling on Laydin-locs grandma trying to take her home with her. "You're coming home with me, and you are going to cook my food, bake me some cookies, read to me, and be my grandma!" insisted the little girl as she continued to tug grandma's jacket.

"NO, no, oh no, I am Laydin-locs grandma, I only cook for her, bake her cookies and read to her. I am her grandma", cried grandma. "I love her so much please let me go little girl!".

A customer heard the announcement on the loudspeaker for the missing "Grandma" she noticed instantly that the woman the little girl was pulling on matches the description and went to tell the Mall office.

The mall officer rushed over at once with Laydin-Locs by his side.

"Let go of that "Grandma" little girl now she does not belong to you", he demanded. Laydin-locs took a giant leap of joy into her grandma's arms promising to never let go of her hand again.

The Mall officer turned to the little girl and said because you tried to kidnap someone else's grandma, you will have to go home, and go to bed without any dessert.

Laydin-locs and her grandma left the mall happily together, holding hands.

The End

Jacqueline James is a published author who specializes in poetry and children's stories. Jacqueline has a 5-star rating and is well known and respected in her community. Her objective is to educate her readers while entertaining them through her unique style of writing. Jacqueline writing puts great emphasis on diversity and overcoming general stereotypes. Her creativity of brilliance leaves you with a euphoria of peace.

If you would like to read other books written
by Jacqueline James

please visit her website @ rhymes64.weebly.com

Sight Words and definitions

Suggested -Put forward for consideration.

Different-Not the same as another or from each other.

Possibly- Perhaps (used in indicate doubt or hesitancy). Perhaps, maybe.

Kidnapped- take (someone) away illegally by force, abduct carry off, capture seize, snatch.

Promise – a declaration of that one will do a particular thing or that a particular thing will happen. Pledge, vow, guarantee, bond, oath

Arrived-reach a place at the end of s journey or a stage of a journey to come, turn up, get there.

Entrance- an opening such as a door, passage or a gate, that allows access to a place.

Desperately – used to emphasize the extreme degree of something.

Mannequin- a dummy used to display clothes in a store.

Elegant- pleasingly gracefully and stylish in appearance or manner.

Distracted- unable to concentrate because one attention is preoccupied.

Mesmerized – hold the attention of (someone) to the exclusion of all else to transfix.

Instantly – at once, Immediately.

Finally- after a long time, typically, involving difficulty or delay.

Describe- give an account in words of (someone or something) including all of the relevant characteristics, qualities, or events.

Composure- The state of felling of being calm in control of oneself.

Immediately- at one instantly.

Announced- make public and typically formal. A declaration

about a fact, occurrence, or an event.

Attention- notice taken of someone or something as interesting or important.

Informed- having or showing knowledge of a subject of situation.

Insisted- demand something forcefully not accepting refusal.

Continue- persist in an activity or a process.

CPSIA information can be obtained
at www.ICGtesting.com
Printed in the USA
JSHW011930111222
34402JS00009B/244